CoComelon

THE BALLOON BOAT RACE!

Adapted by Maria Le
Ready-to-Read

SIMON SPOTLIGHT

An imprint of Simon & Schuster Children's Publishing Division • New York London Toronto Sydney New Delhi
1230 Avenue of the Americas, New York, New York 10020 • This Simon Spotlight edition December 2023
CoComelon™ & © 2023 Moonbug Entertainment. All Rights Reserved. • All rights reserved, including
the right of reproduction in whole or in part in any form. • SIMON SPOTLIGHT, READY-TO-READ, and
colophon are registered trademarks of Simon & Schuster, Inc. • For information about special discounts for
bulk purchases, please contact Simon & Schuster Special Sales at 1-866-506-1949
or business@simonandschuster.com.
Manufactured in the United States of America 1023 LAK • 10 9 8 7 6 5 4 3 2 1
ISBN 978-1-6659-4394-9 (hc) • ISBN 978-1-6659-4393-2 (pbk) • ISBN 978-1-6659-4395-6 (ebook)

Here is a list of all the words you will find in this book. Sound them out before you begin reading the story.

Names:

JJ

TomTom

YoYo

Word families:

"-o"	→	go	so
"-oat"	→	boat	
"-ow"		blow	

Sight words:

a	and	for	help	her
his	is	it	much	one
the	three	time	to	two
up	was	which	will	your

Bonus words:

adds	asks	balloon	friend
fun	race	sail	water
wheels	win	wins	

Ready to go? Happy reading!

Don't miss the questions about the story
on the last page of this book.

It is time for the balloon boat race.

Blow, blow, blow your balloon up.

Which balloon boat will win?

Three, two, one,
and go, go, go!

YoYo's balloon
boat wins the race.

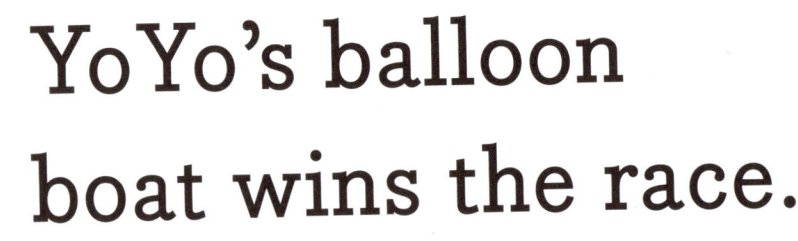

Blow, blow, blow your balloon up.

Which balloon boat will win the race?

TomTom's balloon
boat wins the race!

YoYo adds a sail to her balloon boat.

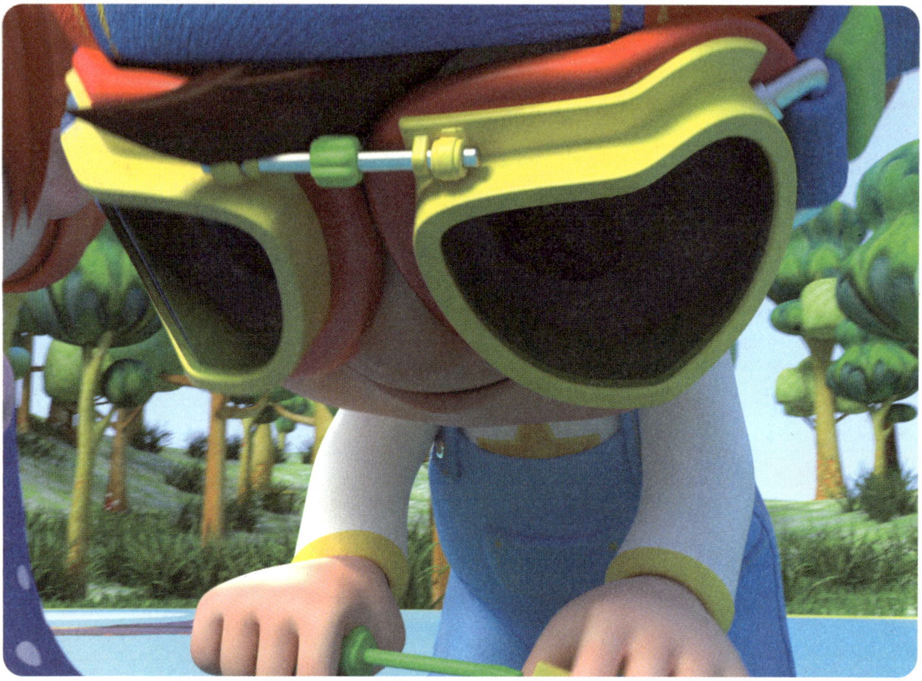

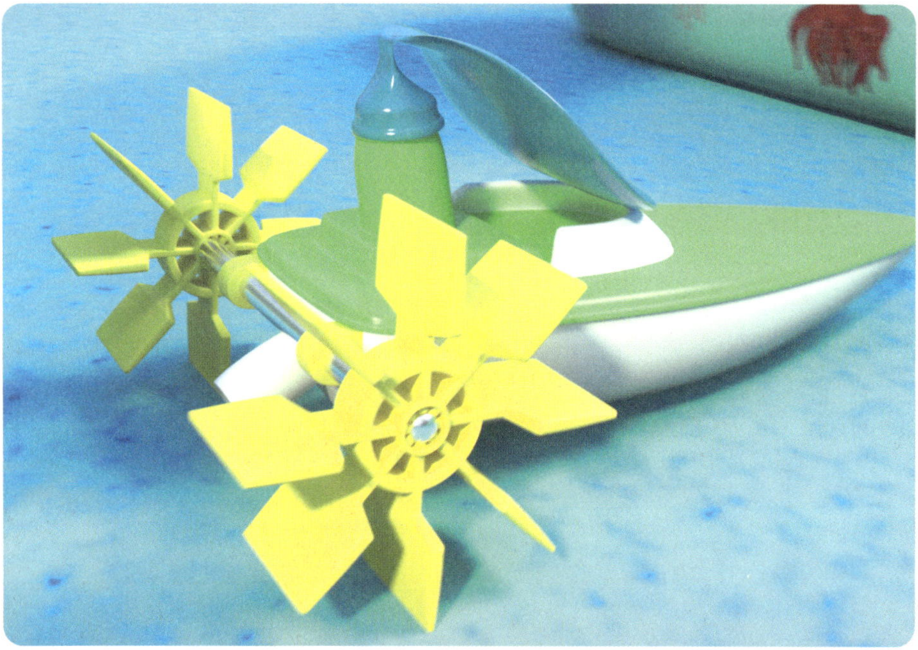

TomTom adds water wheels to his balloon boat.

JJ asks a
friend for help.

Three, two, one,
and go, go, go!

JJ's balloon boat wins the race!

The balloon boat race was so much fun!

Now that you have read the story, can you answer these questions?

1. Which character wins the first balloon boat race? Which character wins the second balloon boat race?

2. How does JJ win the balloon boat race?

3. In this story you read the words "blow" and "go" and "so." Those words rhyme. Can you think of other words that rhyme with "blow" and "go" and "so?"

Great job!
You are a reading star!